How Elephants Lost their Wings

Retold by Lesley Sims
Illustrated by Katie Lovell

This story is all about

flying elephants,

two gods,

some houses,

proud peacocks

and banana trees.

You may not believe me
but, once upon a time,
elephants could fly.

And fly they did.

They flew all over
the jungle.

They soared high into the sky...

...and zoomed down to the ground.

They

even

looped

the

loop.

Sometimes, the gods
went along for a ride.

They sailed through the sky on an elephant's back.

But the elephants were noisy.

They trumpeted, and crowed like roosters.

Cock-a-doodle-do!

Trees and houses shivered and shook,
and shuddered and juddered below them.

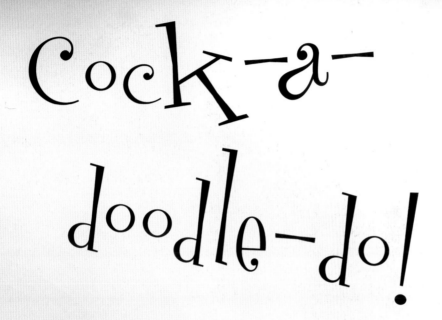

Careless elephants slammed into trees and **snapped** their trunks in two.

They bashed and
crashed into houses...

...and often fell right through.

Soon, all the trees
were bent and broken...

...and the houses were
smashed to smithereens.

"We must stop them," sighed the gods, and they thought of a trick.

They invited every elephant
to a glorious, fruity feast.
How those elephants slurped
and guzzled.

They
chomped...

...and they
gobbled.

And then, when at last their tummies were full, they slept.

While the elephants were snoring,
the gods whisked away their wings.

They gave some to the peacocks,
to wear as splendid tails.

And they stuck some on
banana trees, giving them
huge green leaves.

When the elephants woke up,

they...

were...

FURIOUS!

They shouted
and they stomped,
until the whole
jungle quaked.

But their wings
were gone **forever**.

And they never flew again.

"How Elephants Lost their Wings" is based on a folk tale from India.

Designed by Caroline Spatz and Lenka Hrehova

This edition first published in 2015 by Usborne Publishing Ltd., Usborne House, 83-85 Saffron Hill,
London EC1N 8RT, England. www.usborne.com Copyright © 2015, 2009 Usborne Publishing Ltd.